Ms. Pollywog's Problem-Solving Service

ready, set, read!
FIRST CHAPTER BOOKS

Ms. Pollywog's Problem-Solving Service

Ellen Javernick

Illustrated by Meredith Johnson

Augsburg

MINNEAPOLIS

To my friends in SCBWI
and in my Critique Group

MS. POLLYWOG'S PROBLEM-SOLVING SERVICE

Cover design: Hedstrom Blessing

Library of Congress Cataloging-in-Publication Data
Javernick, Ellen
    Ms. Pollywog's problem-solving service / Ellen Javernick; illustrated by Meredith Johnson.
        p.   cm. — (Ready, set, read! First chapter books)
    Summary: Polly tackles problems of all sizes and with the help of a mystery client, an Afro-American classmate, she even solves the loneliness of a new girl at school.
    ISBN 0-8066-2813-8
    [1. Problem solving—Fiction.   2. Schools—Fiction.   3. Afro-Americans—Fiction.]   I. Johnson, Meredith, ill.   II. Title. III. Series.
PZ7.J329Ms   1995
[Fic]—dc20   95-1188
                                                                         CIP
                                                                          AC

The paper used in this publication meets the minimum requirements of American National Standard for Information Sciences—Permanence of Paper for Printed Library Materials, ANSI Z329.48-1984.   ∞™

Manufactured in the U.S.A.   AF 9-2813
99   98   97   96   95   1   2   3   4   5   6   7   8   9   10

Contents

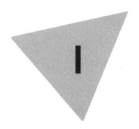

The Make-Believe Monster

"Whaa, whaa, whaa." Polly put her hands over her ears. It didn't help. Joey cried harder. Polly took her hands off her ears. She glared at Joey. "Tomorrow is Mad Minute Day. I have to study multiplication. Stop crying and go to bed."

"I can't go to bed," said Joey. "There's a monster under it."

Polly looked up from her flash cards. "Monsters are just in your imagination." Imagination was one of Polly's favorite words. Ms. Johnston said Polly had a good imagination.

"Monsters aren't just in my imagination," said Joey. "Monsters are real, and there is one under my bed."

Polly shook her head. Her braids bounced. "Boy, are you silly. I suppose he's fuzzy with long, filthy fangs."

Joey stamped his foot. He looked like Thumper the Rabbit in his slipper-footed pj's. "Stop, stop, stop. You're making fun of me. You can't see monsters."

"You can't?"

"No way. Monsters are invisible."

Polly put down her flash cards. "Does it growl? Grrrr, grrrr, grrrr."

Joey shook his head.

"Or roar? Rrrrr, rrrrr, rrrrr."

Joey shook his head harder.

"Or screech?" Polly chased Joey around, screeching "Eeek, eeek, eeek."

"Monsters don't make any noise," said Joey. Then he started to cry.

Mother hurried down the hall. "Polly, get that math finished," she said. She scooped Joey up. "Come on, kiddo. Polly's got work to do."

"I know all these," said Polly. She pointed to a big stack of flash cards.

"You're getting there," said Mother. "But I bet you don't know seven times seven."

Polly hesitated. "Forty-two."

"Try again," Mom encouraged.

"Forty-nine."

"Right. Practice ten more minutes, and then we'll read the next chapter in your *Mrs. Piggle Wiggle* book."

After Mom left with Joey, Polly tried studying problems in her "Not Sure" stack. Even with the door closed, she could hear Joey begging Mom to let him sleep on the couch.

If he doesn't go to bed, thought Polly, I won't get to read with Mom. Polly wondered how Mrs. Piggle Wiggle would solve the problem of the make-believe monster. Suddenly she had an idea.

She jumped up and ran down to the bathroom. Under the sink she found a spray bottle—the one she used to spray her fern. She filled it with water.

Then she went back to her desk. She pulled a piece of paper from her bottom drawer. She looked through the stuff in the top drawer until she found a marker. It was purple, and it didn't write very well. Polly wet it with her tongue. She wrote "Monster Removr" on the paper. She looked at what she'd written. It didn't look quite right. She remembered Ms. Johnston's rule—a vowel for each syllable. She squeezed in a tiny "e" between the "v" in "Removr." Then she taped the paper around the bottle.

She opened the bedroom door. "Joey," she called. "Come see what I found."

Joey came running. He looked at the bottle Polly was holding. "What's that?"

"Monster Remover. You spray it under your bed to make monsters go away."

"Really?" asked Joey.

"It's guaranteed," said Polly. "Let's go test it out right now."

Joey took the monster remover back to his bedroom. He pulled up the bedspread. He squeezed the handle—squirt, squirt, squirt.

"Is the monster gone yet?"

Joey peeked under the bed.

"I don't see anything."

Polly didn't remind Joey that he'd said the monster was invisible. She put her finger to her lips.

Joey listened. "I don't hear anything."

Polly didn't remind Joey that he'd said the monster didn't make any noise. "I guess he must be gone."

"He is," said Joey.

"Great," said Polly. "Now you can go to bed. I'll put the Monster Remover on your little table in case another monster ever shows up."

Joey snuggled down under his covers to wait for Mom to come say prayers and tuck him in.

Later, after her story, Polly snuggled under her own covers. She thought about how she'd solved Joey's problem. Just before she drifted off to sleep a seed of an idea began to form.

Hold the Mayo

By morning Polly's little idea had grown into a big idea. "I'll start a problem-solving service," she told Mandy Sue as they rode the bus together to school. "Just like Mrs. Piggle Wiggle."

Mandy Sue opened her lunch box and wrinkled her nose. "Mayonnaise again. Why can't Mother remember? It's Michael who likes mayonnaise."

Polly kept right on planning. "I better make a list." She pulled a pencil and a piece of squished-up paper from her back-pack. She flattened it out and wrote,

Advertise

"We could make signs," said Mandy Sue, "and put them around the school like they do for Student Council elections."

"Signs," wrote Polly. "And I need a neat name."

"What about Mrs. Polly Wiggle?"

"You've got to be married to be a Mrs.," said Polly. "I'll be a Ms., and I don't want to be Ms. Polly Wiggle. That's almost like copying."

"How about Pollywog—like your dad calls you."

"Perfect," said Polly. "Ms. Pollywog's Problem-Solving Service."

At school Polly told Ms. Johnston about her plan. Ms. Johnston gave her the thumbs-up, good-thinking sign. She let Polly and Mandy Sue stay in at recess to make signs. She helped them write all the words in grown-up spelling. "You may staple them on the bulletin boards," she said.

When the other kids went to computers, Sue put up the signs.

MS. POLLYWOG'S
PROBLEM-SOLVING SERVICE
No problem too small!
No problem too big!

Look for Polly Polanski on the
playground or call her at home 555-8122
before 8.

Polly added the "before eight" because she didn't want kids bothering her mom and dad after she went to bed.

"I bet you'll get lots of business," said Mandy Sue.

When Polly got home, she put a paper tablet on the telephone table. Every time the phone rang, she answered, "Ms. Pollywog's Problem-Solving Service." But the phone was never for her.

Just before bedtime Mandy Sue called. "How many problems have you solved?"

"None," said Polly. "Nobody's called."

"They will," said Mandy Sue. "In the meantime, you can practice on me. You can solve the mayonnaise problem."

Polly plopped down into the big chair. She pulled her feet up under her and rested the phone on her shoulder. Solving problems could take time. "What have you tried already?"

"I've reminded Mom millions of times," said Mandy Sue. "And I've stuck 'Hold the Mayo' notes on my lunch box, but she still gets mixed up and puts mayonnaise sandwiches in my lunch box instead of Michael's."

"Hmm," said Polly. She wrote "mayo" on the paper tablet. "Have you thought about making your own sandwiches?"

"No," said Mandy Sue.

"Well, I think that's the solution. My grandma has a plaque on her wall that says, 'God sends every bird its food, but he doesn't throw it into the nest.' I think it means you have to do things for yourself. I bet your mom will be glad to have you take over."

"It's worth a try," said Mandy Sue.

After Mandy Sue said good night, Polly wrote:

Name of client	Problem	Solution
Joey Polanski	Monster under bed	Monster Spray
Mandy Sue Wilson	Misplaced mayo	Make own lunch

Bothersome Baby

"I made my own lunch," said Mandy Sue. She slid into the seat beside Polly.

"Without mayo on your sandwich?"

"You bet! You know, I've been thinking," said Mandy Sue. "Maybe kids think they have to pay to get their problems solved. That might be why you haven't had any other clients."

"I didn't think of that," said Polly.

As soon as first bell rang, Polly and Mandy Sue rushed in to squeeze in the words "No Charge" on the signs.

Mandy stepped back from the last sign. "Do you think the little kids will know that 'No Charge' means free?"

MS. POLLYWOG'S
PROBLEM-SOLVING SERVICE
No problem too small!
No problem too big!
No CHARGE!
Look for Polly Polanski on the
playground or call her at home 555-8122
before 8.

"Oh gosh," Polly moaned. "They probably can't read my signs at all."

"Maybe Mr. Raisch will let us make an announcement."

Polly and Mandy Sue hurried down to the office.

"Leave your sign here," said Mr. Raisch. "I'll have a sixth grader read it after the flag salute." He pointed to the office door. "You girls go back to class so Ms. Johnston won't mark you tardy."

Polly got to 3A just in time to hear her announcement over the loudspeaker. She could hardly wait till recess. Maybe there would be a client looking for her. She took her paper tablet out with her. She and

20

Mandy Sue walked all around the playground, but nobody came with a problem.

After recess it was the time Ms. Johnston's class read with their first-grade partners. Polly always read with Jason Dreith. Today Jason asked her to read *A.J. Flips*. He pointed to the picture of A.J. "She's just like my little brother."

"Oh?" said Polly.

"Richie always wants to play with whatever I'm playing with."

"You have a problem," said Polly. "I will help you solve it."

"I can't solve it. If I don't give Richie my toys, he cries and I get in trouble," said Jason in a loud voice.

"Use your four-inch voices, please," said Mrs. Johnston. She looked right at Polly and Jason.

"Wait a sec," whispered Polly. She tiptoed to her desk and came back with her paper tablet and a pencil.

"So what do you do when Richie grabs your toys?"

"I have to let him have them."

Polly thought a minute. "Have you tried closing the door to your room?"

"It's his room too, so I have to let him in."

"Oh, " said Polly. What had she done when Joey was a baby and wanted to play with her toys? She remembered. She'd given him something else to play with. She remembered that even God didn't always give people what they prayed for.

Polly patted Jason's shoulder. "This is what you're going to do," she whispered.

"Ding, ding, ding." Ms. Johnston was ringing the end-of-reading bell.

Polly talked fast. "When Richie gets ready to grab something, give him another toy. That will make him happy."

Jason hurried to line up. "I'll try it," he called over his shoulder.

Polly filled in her tablet.

Name of client	Problem	Solution
Joey Polanski	Monster under bed	Monster Spray
Mandy Sue Wilson	Misplaced mayo	Make own lunch
Jason Dreith	Bothersome baby	Substitute something

She wondered who would need her help next.

When the phone rang after supper, Polly answered, "Ms. Pollywog's Problem-Solving Service. Polly speaking."

Polly heard a click. How very strange. She waited by the phone. Maybe the caller would call back. Maybe the caller would come over. But the caller did not call back, and nobody came over.

The Bully at the Bus Stop

The next morning on the bus Polly told Mandy Sue about the strange hang-up call. "Do you suppose it could have been a client?" asked Mandy Sue.

"It might have been."

"Excuse me," said the girl in the seat behind Polly.

Polly leaned over to look through the crack between the seats.

"Are you the real Ms. Pollywog?"

Polly giggled. "In person. Do you have a problem?"

"Well, sort of. I'm Kimi Matsunaka. My little sister's in 1C. She told me to talk to you about the bully at our bus stop."

Polly got up on her knees and leaned over the back of the seat so she and Kimi could talk better. "What does he do to bother you?"

"He says he's going to beat us up if we don't bring him popcorn every day."

"Do you bring it?" asked Polly.

"Wouldn't you?"

"Polly Polanski," the bus driver's voice boomed over the loudspeaker. "Sit down this minute!"

Polly's face got hot. She turned around and sat down. She took out her tablet and added Kimi's name and problem to her list. She didn't write down a solution because she didn't have one yet. She wrote a note. It said:

Look For me at lunch.

She slipped it to Kimi through the crack between the seats.

All morning Polly pretended to be doing her work, but she was thinking about Kimi's problem. Maybe I could make them bully-proof vests. That sounds good, but

26

vests probably wouldn't help. You couldn't always ignore bullies. Sometimes you had to stand up to them. Polly's father said you had to stand up without fighting back. That was hard. Polly wished she could do magic like Mrs. Piggle Wiggle. Suddenly she remembered that most magic was just tricks. She knew how they could play a trick on the bus-stop bully.

"Please pass up your papers," said Ms. Johnston.

Polly had done only two problems, but she passed her paper up anyway. She crossed her fingers. She hoped Ms. Johnston wouldn't want her to finish at lunch. Luckily, Ms. Johnson didn't even look at the papers.

Kimi was waiting when third grade came out for lunch recess.

Polly explained her plan. "Just get to your bus stop early. I'll meet you there with a bag of special bully-buster popcorn."

After supper, Jason called to tell Polly how he'd fooled Richie. "He didn't cry at all when I gave him a stuffed monkey instead of my remote-control car."

Polly was glad she didn't get any other calls that night. She needed time to get things ready. First she popped popcorn. She had to pop two batches because Joey and her dad smelled it cooking and wanted some.

Polly filled a brown lunch sack full of fresh-popped corn. Then she got the garlic salt from the cupboard. She sprinkled it on the popcorn. Then she sprinkled on some of the hot pepper her dad used when he made chili. Just a little, thought Polly, not too much. She sniffed the popcorn. Her eyes began to water. Quickly she closed the top of the sack. Perfect!

In the morning Polly and Joey walked two extra blocks to Kimi's bus stop. Polly gave Kimi the popcorn. Then they all waited for the bus and the bully.

The bully got there just as the bus drove up. He slipped up beside Kimi. "Where's my popcorn?" he whispered.

"You really don't want this popcorn," said Kimi.

"Give it to me now or I'm going to beat you up," commanded the bully. Joey moved closer to Polly.

The bully grabbed the sack of popcorn right out of Kimi's hand.

"You'll be sorry if you eat it," warned Polly.

The bully paid no attention. He pushed ahead of them. He went way to the back of the bus. Kimi and Polly and Joey sat together right behind the bus driver. They looked straight ahead.

The bus had just stopped at the school when the bully came rushing to the front door. He was fanning his face.

"Water! Water!" he shouted. "Let me out. I need water."

The door swung open, and the bully rushed into the building.

"I bet he won't bother you for popcorn again," said Polly. She got out her paper tablet and filled in the solution column.

Name of client	Problem	Solution
Joey Polanski	Monster under bed	Monster Spray
Mandy Sue Wilson	Misplaced mayo	Make own lunch
Jason Dreith	Bothersome baby	Substitute something
Kimi Matsunaka	Bus-stop bully	Pepper popcorn

5

Simple Arithmetic

"Hi, Mom, I'm home," called Polly. She tossed her backpack onto a chair.

"Somebody just called for you, dear," said Mrs. Polanski. "I wrote his name on the pad by the phone."

Polly hurried to look at the name her mother had written:

Tim Beckman 555-2088

"He insisted it was an emergency," said Mrs. Polanski, "and said you should call right away."

Polly didn't stop to eat the snack Mother had set out for her. Oatmeal cookies could wait. It didn't sound as if her client could.

Polly dialed the number her mom had written.

"I'm glad you called," said Tim. "I sure hope you can help, but you probably can't 'cause you're only in third grade."

"I can try," said Polly. "But I can't help if you don't tell me the problem."

"I don't have much time," said Tim. "I'm supposed to be at soccer practice, but Mom said I can't go till I know my multiplication facts."

"Don't you know any of them?" asked Polly.

"Of course I do," said Tim. "Actually, the only ones I have trouble with are the nines."

"Are you ever in luck," said Polly. "My Uncle Peter showed me a simple way to do nines. He learned it when he was in Japan."

"Tell me the trick," begged Tim.

"It's too hard to tell over the phone. I'll have to show you."

Tim groaned. "Mom said I couldn't leave until I could give the answers as fast as she could give the problems."

"Hmm," said Polly. "How about if I come to your house? Florists and book-mobiles deliver. Pizza places deliver. I can deliver too!"

"Oh, would you?" Tim sounded relieved. "I live two houses down from your friend Mandy Sue. That's how I found out about your problem-solving service."

"I'm on my way," said Polly. She explained to Mom where she was going, grabbed her cookies, and dashed out the door.

Tim was waiting on his steps. "So what's the secret?"

"It's easier to show with a pen," said Polly.

Tim ran inside to get one.

Polly put her hands out in front of her on the step. She took the pen and wrote numbers on her fingers. "Ask me a problem."

"Nine times four," said Tim.

Polly pulled her "number four" finger back. Before Tim had time to ask what she was doing, Polly said, "Thirty-six."

"Are you sure?" asked Tim.

"Sure I'm sure," said Polly. "Give me another one."

"I'll check you on this one," said Tim. "I already know the answer. Nine times five."

"Cinchy." Polly flicked down her "number five" finger. "Forty-five."

"Wow!" said Tim. "You're right, but how do you do it?"

"Watch," said Polly. "I put down the finger that matches the number I'm multiplying by nine. When you say nine times five, I push down my fifth finger. Then I look at the fingers that are still up. There are four fingers before the pushed-down one, so four's the number in the 'tens' column. There are five fingers after the pushed-down one. That's the number in the 'ones' column. So the answer is forty-five."

"Let me try," said Tim. He put his own hands out on the step. "For nine times seven, I push down my seventh finger. There are six fingers on the left and three on the right, so the answer's sixty-three."

"You've got it!" said Polly. "Now practice a bit before you show your mom."

Tim tried the trick a couple of times, then he called, "Mom, come ask me my nines."

Mrs. Beckman came to the door. "Nine times eight."

"Seventy-two," shouted Tim.

"Nine times three."

"Twenty-seven. Now may I go to practice?" Tim begged.

Mrs. Beckman nodded. "But before you leave, tell me how you learned your facts so fast."

Tim jumped on his skateboard and started down the sidewalk. "Ask Polly," he called.

"I've been trying to teach Tim for weeks," said Mrs. Beckman. "How did you do it in just ten minutes?"

Polly stood up. "I explained it in a way Tim could understand. You know, like in the Bible when Jesus explained stuff with stories."

"Well, we certainly thank you," said Mrs. Beckman.

Polly handed her the pen. "I'd better be going. Somebody else may need help with a problem." When she waved goodbye, Polly noticed that she still had numbers on her fingers. She'd have to remember to wash!

The Big Bragger

When the phone rang during dinner, Polly had to let the answering machine take it. Dinner didn't get interrupted at the Polanski's.

Later when Polly listened to the machine, there weren't any messages. "Oh rats. It must have been my mystery caller."

"How many problems have you solved?" asked Joey.

"Five, if I count your monster."

"You're getting famous. All my friends know about you. I told Elizabeth Watkins she should come over after supper and you'd solve her problem."

When Elizabeth rang the bell, Polly was ready. She'd made a nameplate for the dining room table.

PoLLY PoLANSKi

Her tablet and pencil were out.

"Hi, " said Elizabeth. "I hope you can help. It's my brother, Andy. He's the biggest bragger in the whole wide world."

"Sit down and tell me more," said Polly.

"He always says that he's got more raisins in his cereal, that his shoes are faster, and that Fluffy—she's our cat—likes him better. He brags 'cause his bike's bigger and his library books are longer."

"Bragging's not nice," said Polly. "It says so in the Bible."

"But he does it anyway," said Elizabeth. "Everything I can do, he says he can do better."

"But of course that's not true," said Polly.

Elizabeth shook her head. "No, but when I tell him that, he always argues. Then Mom hears us and gets mad at me."

Polly got up. She paced around the table. "You do have a problem, but we can solve it. Arguing is not the answer. Andy can't argue without you. It takes two."

"So what should I do?" asked Elizabeth.

"Always agree."

Elizabeth wrinkled her nose.

"It works every time," said Polly. She plunked back down into her chair. "It won't be easy though. It sounds like Andy's pretty good at getting your goat."

"Goat? I haven't got a goat."

Polly giggled. "That just means he's good at getting you mad. But we can fool him. In Sunday school sometimes we give little plays so we can learn how to get along with other kids. Mrs. Olsen calls it role-playing."

Polly raised her voice. "Hey, Joey," she called. "Come here a minute."

Joey poked his head into the dining room. "What do you want?"

"You've got to play the father. I'll act like Andy, and Elizabeth will be herself. If she starts arguing with me, you have to scold her."

"I'd rather be a dinosaur than a dad," complained Joey. He made a few dinosaur noises. "Rhhhhhh, rhhhhhh."

Polly gave Joey her best I'll-get-you-if-you-don't-do-it look. She pointed to a chair. "Sit there and pretend you're reading the paper."

"OK, OK," said Joey.

Polly turned to Elizabeth. "My hair's prettier than your hair. It's much prettier than yours."

Elizabeth patted her hair with her hands. "No, it's not. Red's just as pretty as blond, and besides, my hair's shinier."

"It's not." Polly sounded like she was going to cry. She poked Joey.

Joey pretended not to notice.

"Daddy, Daddy," wailed Polly. "Elizabeth says her hair's shinier than mine."

Joey looked up from his make-believe paper.

"Elizabeth, stop that teasing this very minute." He shook his finger. "Or you'll go straight to your room."

Polly made an X with her arms. "Cut! See how you got in trouble even though I started it?"

Elizabeth nodded.

"Let's try again," said Polly. "Except this time just agree with me. You'll see what happens."

Polly disappeared into the kitchen. She came back with a plate of chocolate-chip cookies. She put one in front of herself and gave one to Elizabeth. "I've got more chips in my cookie," she bragged.

Elizabeth looked at her cookie. She started to answer.

"Remember," said Polly.

"That's true," said Elizabeth. "I guess you do."

"My cookie's bigger than yours," said Polly.

Elizabeth looked at the cookies. They were both the same size. Polly nudged her before she could say so.

Elizabeth faked a sweet smile. "I think you're right. Yours really is bigger."

Polly tried again. "Mine's softer."

Elizabeth didn't even need a reminder this time. She played her part perfectly. She patted Polly's cookie and pronounced, "It certainly *is* softer!"

Polly clapped. "Great acting. Now you just have to remember to act the same way when Andy brags."

"I'll try," promised Elizabeth.

Polly gave Joey a cookie. "Thanks for helping," she said.

"And thank you for helping me," said Elizabeth as she and Polly walked to the front door.

Polly waved good-bye. She was turning to go back inside when she saw a note

taped to the door. A silly, scared-looking
rabbit was drawn in the corner.

The note said:

Polly,
I need your help. Meet
me by the big slide
before school tomorrow.

Messy Jessy

"Nobody came," said Polly. "But maybe whoever wrote it was absent today. I'll wait by the slide again tomorrow."

Mandy Sue headed down the aisle to get off the bus. "Maybe," she called over her shoulder, "your mystery client meant the kindergarten slide."

Polly got out the note to check. She almost didn't notice the tall girl who slipped into the seat beside her.

"You're Polly, right?"

Polly nodded.

"I'm Maria Garcia. Tim Beckman told about how you helped him learn his nines, and I thought maybe you could help me."

Polly pointed to the note on her lap. "Did you write this?"

"Not me. I'm in fourth grade. I can write better than that."

Polly put the note back into her backpack and pulled out her tablet. "Well, how can I help you?"

"I have to share a room with my big sister," said Maria. "And she's a slob. I can't study because my desk is covered with her stuff. I've even got to throw her underwear off my bed before I can get into it."

"Boy," said Polly. "Your sister sounds even messier than I am. Couldn't you move to another room?"

Maria shook her head. "There are just two bedrooms in our house."

"I suppose you told your mom."

"I did," said Maria, "but even when Mama makes Jessy pick up, the room never stays clean."

"Oh my!" Polly grabbed her backpack. "I've got to go. This is my stop. I'll get back to you tomorrow."

"I hope you think of something," called Maria.

After supper Polly knitted on the scarf she was making for the church bazaar. She thought about Maria's problem. "Brrring, brrrring," the phone rang. When she jumped up to get it, the ball of red yarn fell to the floor and rolled across the room. "Give me a break," said Polly. She picked up the phone. "Hello, Ms. Pollywog's Problem-Solving Service."

"Oh," said a voice. "I must have the wrong number."

Polly put down the phone and started rerolling the red yarn. Suddenly she remembered the Bible story about how God divided the Red Sea. I have it, she thought. I know how to solve Maria's messy-room problem. Polly got out her scissors. She cut a long length of red yarn. She put it with her lunch so she wouldn't forget it in the morning.

The next day Maria had saved Polly a seat on the bus. "Did you think of something?"

"I sure did," said Polly. She opened her backpack. "Yuck!" Her tuna sandwich was already beginning to smell. "I bet this will work," she said as she pulled out the yarn.

"What am I supposed to do with it?" asked Maria.

"Take it home and unroll it right down the middle of your bedroom. Move all Jessy's junk to one side. Tell her she can be a slob on her side, but that she can't mess up your side."

"It sounds kind of silly, but I'll try anything." Maria very carefully tucked the yarn into her jacket pocket.

Polly filled in her case log.

Name of client	Problem	Solution
Joey Polanski	Monster under bed	Monster Spray
Mandy Sue Wilson	Misplaced mayo	Make own lunch
Jason Dreith	Bothersome baby	Substitute something

Kimi Matsunaka	Bus-stop bully	Pepper popcorn
Tim Beckman	Knowing the nines	Simple arithmetic
Elizabeth Watkins	Big bragger	Always agree
Maria Garcia	Messy Jessy	Yarn divider

"Say," asked Maria, "did you ever find out which kid wrote that note?"

"Nope," said Polly, "but I'll go wait at the slide again this morning."

The Puppy Problem

When the bus let the kids off in back of the school, Polly hurried to the slide. There were already three kids standing near it.

"Were you waiting for me?" she asked a girl in a white baseball hat. The girl looked down at Polly and shook her head. "I'm just waiting for the soccer game to start."

Polly went up to one of the boys. "Did you leave me a note?"

The boy gave Polly a strange look. "Not me."

His voice sounded familiar, but Polly didn't remember meeting him. "Do I know you?" she asked. The boy shook his head and moved away from the slide. Polly noticed that he was carrying a sketch pad. He must like drawing.

The only person still by the slide was another boy Polly knew from church. "Hi, Chris. Did you leave a note on my door?"

"A note? Why, no," said Chris.

Polly told Chris all about her Problem-Solving Service.

"Hey, cool!" said Chris. "It must be neat to help people just like Jesus did. Say, maybe you can even help me. Do you solve problems with pets?"

"I never have," said Polly. "But I can try. What's the matter?"

Chris pulled a picture from his pocket and handed it to Polly. "This is Zeppy. We just got her. Isn't she a cute puppy?"

Polly nodded. "Adorable!"

"Well, here's the problem. Zeppy cries all night 'cause she doesn't like to stay alone in the kitchen."

Polly handed the picture back. "Can't you let her sleep in your room?"

"Mom says no because she still makes puddles. We called the pet store, and they suggested putting an alarm clock in with her. It didn't work though."

"Hmm," said Polly. "I don't know much about puppies. Dad and Mom got our dog, Grover, before I was even born."

"Clang, clang." Second bell sounded. Polly and Chris headed for their lines. "I'll think of a plan," Polly promised. She looked back at the slide. No one was there.

When it was library time, Polly typed *P-E-T* into the computer catalog. In seconds a long list of pet books showed up on the screen. Most of them had the same number—636. Polly searched the shelves until she found the 636s. Some of the books looked hard to read. At last she found one called *How to Take Care of Your Puppy*. It had big letters and lots of pictures. She took it to the check-out desk.

"Did you get another dog?" whispered Mandy Sue.

Polly shook her head. She explained about Chris's problem. " 'A smart person,' she quoted her mom, 'may not have all the answers. She just knows how to find them.' I didn't know much about dogs, but I did know how to learn more."

At the reading table, Polly looked at the titles of the chapters. One was *Helping Your Puppy Feel at Home.* Polly turned to it. She read:

> At first your puppy may cry at night. He feels like you would feel in a strange place. Try a loud alarm clock. Put it near where your puppy sleeps. The tick-tock of the clock will sound like the mother dog's heart beating.

Polly remembered that Chris had already tried the clock. She read on:

> If that doesn't do the trick, maybe your puppy is missing you. Let your puppy sleep on something you've worn.

Polly didn't have to read the rest of the chapter. Now she had a plan.

54

After lunch she waited to tell Chris about it. Maria came by. "Jessy's just as messy, but it's not so bad now that I have my own space."

"Glad to help," said Polly. She waved to Chris. "Over here!"

"That makes sense," said Chris when Polly told him what the book said. "I'll let Zeppy sleep on my T-shirt tonight."

"I would never have thought of it myself," said Polly.

"Only God knows everything." Chris waved good-bye. "I hope you find out who put the note on your door."

The Mystery Client

Next morning Polly climbed to the top of the slide. I'll sit here, she thought. Maybe my mystery client didn't see me those other days.

Elizabeth stopped at the slide on her way to play four-square. "It worked! You should have seen Andy's face when I agreed that his muscles were bigger than mine." Elizabeth giggled. "He kept opening and closing his mouth like a fish. He couldn't think of any way to argue with me."

"Glad I could help," said Polly.

Someone poked Polly in the back. "Are you going to sit there all day?"

"Gosh, I'm sorry," said Polly. "I didn't notice that anyone was waiting." Swoosh! She started down the slide. Smash! She crashed into somebody. It was the boy she'd talked to at the slide the day before. He seemed OK, but Polly's nose was bleeding.

"Sorry," said the boy.

"It was my fault," said Polly. She felt sort of shaky, but she didn't cry. "Do you suppose you could walk me to the nurse's office?"

"Oh, sure." The boy picked up his sketch pad. "My name's Malcolm. Malcolm Harris. I'm in third grade." Malcolm handed Polly a facial tissue. "It's clean."

"I'm Polly Polanski," said Polly as they started toward the school. Only because she was using the facial tissue, it came out "Polly Bolanski."

"We had a crash," Malcolm explained to Mrs. Ochs.

Mrs. Ochs pointed to the little refrigerator. "Get Polly an ice pack, and I'll be

in to check on her when I finish selling lunch tickets."

Malcolm got a blue ice bag. He handed it to Polly and sat down on the plastic cot beside her.

"Show me your pictures," said Polly. "It will keep my mind off the blood."

"Sure," said Malcolm. He opened his sketch pad.

Polly turned the pages. "You're really good at drawing," she said. Suddenly something caught her eye. There was the same silly, scared rabbit that had been on the note from her mystery client.

"You wrote the note?"

Malcolm nodded. "I even called you a couple of times on the phone."

"But why?"

"Because I've got a problem," said Malcolm. "But it might be too big for you."

"No problem too big," Polly quoted. "No problem too small. What's the trouble?"

"I'm shy," said Malcolm, "I'm just like the rabbit in this picture. That's why I hung up before I talked to you on the phone."

Polly took the ice bag off her nose. The bleeding started again. She put it back. "You don't seem shy with me."

"That's because I know you now," said Malcolm.

"Well, you can't go around waiting for people to bump into you. Besides, being shy isn't bad," said Polly. "Some people just make friends faster than others. Anyway, I think you already know how to solve your problem."

"I do?" Malcolm looked puzzzled.

"You show yourself to others bit by bit." Polly pointed to Malcolm's sketch book. "You're like the rabbit. When he feels safe, he hops out."

Malcolm pulled a pencil from his backpack. He drew a happy, hopping rabbit. "This is for you," he said. He handed it to Polly.

"Gee, thanks," said Polly. "God gave you a talent that you shouldn't keep hidden."

Mrs. Ochs hurried into the nurse's office. She checked Polly's nose. "I see the ice pack did the trick. I hope you won't have any more problems."

Polly winked at Malcolm.

"I hope I will."

Making New Friends

On the way back to class, Polly stopped in the girl's bathroom to look in the mirror. She wanted to see if her eyes were turning black. They weren't. Her nose seemed bigger than it had before she bumped into Malcolm, but it didn't look too bad.

She was just heading out the door when she heard crying. The sound was coming from one of the stalls. Polly looked under the door. All she could see was a pair of red sneakers. Suddenly the door opened. Out walked a girl about Polly's size. Her face was almost as red as her sneakers, and she was sobbing.

"Are you sick?" asked Polly.

"No," answered a shaky voice.

"Are you hurt?"

Red Sneakers shook her head.

"I don't think I know you," said Polly.

"That's the . . . sniff, sniff . . . whole problem. At my old school lots of people knew me. Nobody knows me here."

"Well, I'd like to know you," said Polly. "What's your name?"

"Angela Bertotti. Mostly people call me Angie."

"Is this your first day at Edgemont?"

"My third," said Angie. She pulled a paper towel from the roll. "The other days Mrs. Murphy assigned kids to play with me. But now everybody's back to playing with their old friends."

"I'm Polly Polanski. I'm in one of the other third-grade classes," said Polly. "I've gone to Edgemont since kindergarten, but not everybody knows me."

Angie got the paper towel wet. She blotted her red face. "But lots of kids say hi when they see *you* in the hall. They wave to you out of the bus windows. They ask you to play on the playground."

"That is true," said Polly. "I guess it just takes time for people to get to know new kids."

"That's what my mom told me too," said Angie. "In the meantime it's awfully lonely."

"I guess it would be," said Polly. "But I have an idea for a way to get you friends fast."

Angie looked happier.

"We'll have to have help," said Polly. "Look for me at lunch recess."

"Where?" asked Angie.

Polly thought a minute. "The slide is not the safest spot to meet," she said. "How about by the big map on the black-top?"

"I'll be standing on New York," said Angie. "That's where we moved from."

"Super," said Polly. "See you there."

At lunch Polly watched for the rest of the third grade to come into the lunchroom. She waved to Malcolm and motioned him over to her table.

"How's your nose?" asked Malcolm.

Polly had been so busy thinking about how they could solve Angie's problem that she'd forgotten all about her nose. She felt it. "It hardly hurts. I have a problem that I can't solve without you," said Polly. "Will you help?"

"I'll do what I can," said Malcolm.

Polly started to explain, but the lunchroom monitor told Malcolm to move. "Meet me by the map," called Polly.

Polly and Angie were waiting when Malcolm got there. Polly had already learned lots of interesting things about Angie. Angie loved spaghetti. "Me too," said Polly. And her favorite sport was swimming. She hadn't ridden the bus yet, but when she did, it would be bus number twenty-one.

"Malcolm," said Polly, "this is Angie Bertotti. She's new at Edgemont. She wishes more people knew her. I have a great plan for how we can help. We will make 'WANTED' posters. We'll give a prize to everyone who brings us information about Angie. Pretty soon lots of people will know her. What do you think?"

"Great idea, but what do you need me for?" asked Malcolm.

"Polly said that you were super good at drawing," said Angie. "She said you could draw my picture to put on the poster."

Polly pulled a pencil and a piece of paper from her pocket. "I came prepared."

Malcolm looked at the scrunched-up paper. He laughed. "Lucky thing I always carry my sketch pad. Why don't you sit over on the swing, Angie, and I'll draw you."

Malcolm finished just before the third-grade bell rang. He handed the picture to Polly.

"It really looks like you, Angie," said Polly as they hurried to line up.

Next morning Polly came to school with twenty posters. Her dad had driven her down to the library so she could make copies of the original.

<u>WANTED</u>
Information about this person.
What is her name?
Where did she move from?
What is her favorite food?
What is her favorite sport?
What bus does she ride?
When you know the answers
find Polly Polanski and she will
give you a prize.

At first Polly was going to bring gum from her gum bank for the prizes, but Mom thought giving gum might get Polly in trouble. Then Polly remembered the box of 1001 stickers she had gotten for her birthday. She brought them for prizes instead.

Mr. Raisch gave Polly and Malcolm and Angie permission to put up the posters at noon. That meant they got to sit together at lunch. Polly and Angie both had the hot lunch because it was spaghetti day, and they *loved* spaghetti.

Malcolm said, "I guess I earn the first sticker, because I know Angie now and I'll say hi whenever I see her."

"Pretty soon," said Polly, "lots of other kids will know her too."

"Thanks, Polly," said Angie.

"I couldn't have done it without Malcolm," Polly replied.

"No problem," said Malcolm. "It was fun."

Polly laughed. "I hope we can solve lots more problems together, partner."

"I'd like that," Malcolm said.

Polly reached across the lunch table to shake Malcolm's hand. She forgot that she was wearing a dress with long sleeves and she was eating spaghetti. Polly and Malcolm shook hands up and down, up

and down, up and down. With each shake, Polly's sleeve dipped into her spaghetti and flipped sauce onto the front of Malcolm's shirt. In a few seconds his shirt was spotted with spaghetti and her sleeve was wet with sauce.

"Oh, no!" Polly groaned. "We're a mess!"

Malcolm laughed. "Looks like we're the ones with the problem now, Polly. Got any ideas to solve it?"

"It's the messiest problem I've had to solve," said Polly. "But it's the easiest too. The only solution to our spaghetti-clothes problem is plain old soap and water!"

Name of client	Problem	Solution
Joey Polanski	Monster under bed	Monster Spray
Mandy Sue Wilson	Misplaced mayo	Make own lunch
Jason Dreith	Bothersome baby	Substitute Something

Kimi Matsunaka   Bus-stop   Pepper
                 bully   popcorn

Tim Beckman   Knowing the   Simple
              nines   arithmetic

Elizabeth Watkins   Big bragger   Always
                                  agree

Maria Garcia   Messy Jessy   Yarn
                             divider

Chris Davis   Lonely puppy   Something
                             smelly

Malcolm Harris   Shy guy   Give it
                           time

Angie Bertotti   New kid   Advertise

Polly and Malcolm   Spilled   Soap and
                    spaghetti water